EUGENE
at the Christmas Ball with Christine
The Decisions of a Creative Mouse

written by
Lynn C. Skinner

illustrated by
Polly Rushton

Other books in the series by this author

Eugene and His Go-Kart Machine
     A Tale of a Creative Mouse
Eugene's Mistake at the Garden Gate
     The Resolve of a Creative Mouse
Eugene Meets Bojean
     The Acceptance of a Creative Mouse
Eugene, the Mouse, at the Big Farmhouse
     The Contentment of a Creative Mouse

Eugene at the Christmas Ball with Christine
The Decisions of a Creative Mouse

ISBN Number: 9780984734412
Library of Congress Control Number: 2012919332

Copyright 2017
4th printing

Lynn C Skinner
P.O. Box 34
Ailey, GA 30410
www.eugenethemouse.com

This book is dedicated to Truett Andrew, a wonderful and persistent helper. Mrs. Andrew has spent her life and energy communicating, praying, connecting and living for others.

Acknowledgements

During any project, there are often many individuals who help with suggestions or encouragement. Our special thanks to the Listons plus Ed, Robin and Sarah, Amy and Elizabeth for interest and comments.

"Eugene......EUGENE......"

It was a cool, fall day on the farm. The leaves were turning beautiful colors. Eugene, the mouse, had been busy all morning gathering seeds and nuts for his winter storehouse. The activity made him tired, and now he was taking a nap.

EUGENE......

Suddenly Eugene was awake and realized that someone was calling. He ran around the barn to meet his friend Christine.

Christine was so excited that Eugene couldn't understand what she was saying. Finally he convinced her to sit on the tree stump, talk slowly and enunciate so that he could understand her.

Soon Christine departed and Eugene began to worry. Christine had been gathering seeds by the big house and heard the people talking about a Christmas party. The people would wear clothes commemorating southern states before and during the War Between the States. There would be delicious food, glittering decorations and elegant dancing. Christine wanted to attend, but she needed Eugene's help. Would Eugene accompany her?

What to do? WHAT TO DO? This was a huge challenge for Eugene. The food did sound tempting, but a costume would be a problem and dancing! Didn't Christine say dancing?

Eugene tried to return to his nap and forget the entire conversation. However, his mind was racing with thoughts. He didn't want to be selfish. He had learned that it was good to be helpful but...

Finally Eugene had a few ideas.
He ran to check the go-kart which
he had built. The go-kart was ready.
He had solved one problem. They
would drive to the party in his
machine. Now what about a
costume?

This entire idea was becoming complicated. Eugene sat on a stump and began to discuss his dilemma with his friends. The more Eugene talked and balked, the more excited the animals became.

Eugene finally realized that he must help his friend. Christine couldn't go to the party without an escort. He must make the correct decision. What would he wear? He needed to consider his options.

Home Sweet Home

The evening of the party
arrived. Eugene donned his special
tie and went to get Christine.

Eugene and Christine arrived at the party in the go-kart. Excitement was everywhere with guests talking and music playing.

When the food was placed on the table, Eugene and Christine watched for wonderful morsels to be dropped. When the music began, they danced!

To signal the end of the evening, an old canon from the era was fired on the lawn.

  As Eugene returned home, he was happy he had decided to help his friend. He knew in his heart that helping Christine was the correct decision.

Joy
Love
FRIEND

Lynn C. Skinner, author
Polly Rushton, illustrator

As former teachers who continue to be interested in children, Lynn C. Skinner and Polly Rushton formed a friendship with the idea of helping children through creative thought, expanded vocabulary and character building.

We hope that you enjoy this second book in the Eugene the Mouse series.